D0520752

# Elephants Walk Together

CHERYL LAWTON MALONE

pictures by
BISTRA MASSEVA

ALBERT WHITMAN & COMPANY
CHICAGO, ILLINOIS

In the wild,
two baby elephants
walk together.
Eyes bright,
trunks curled,

they forage and roam,
curious and proud,
under a beaming sun.

The first night star shines
on Precious and Baba talking,

and mothers and sisters,
and cousins and brothers.
A noisy family walking.

Until one day,
hunters capture the calves
and send them away.

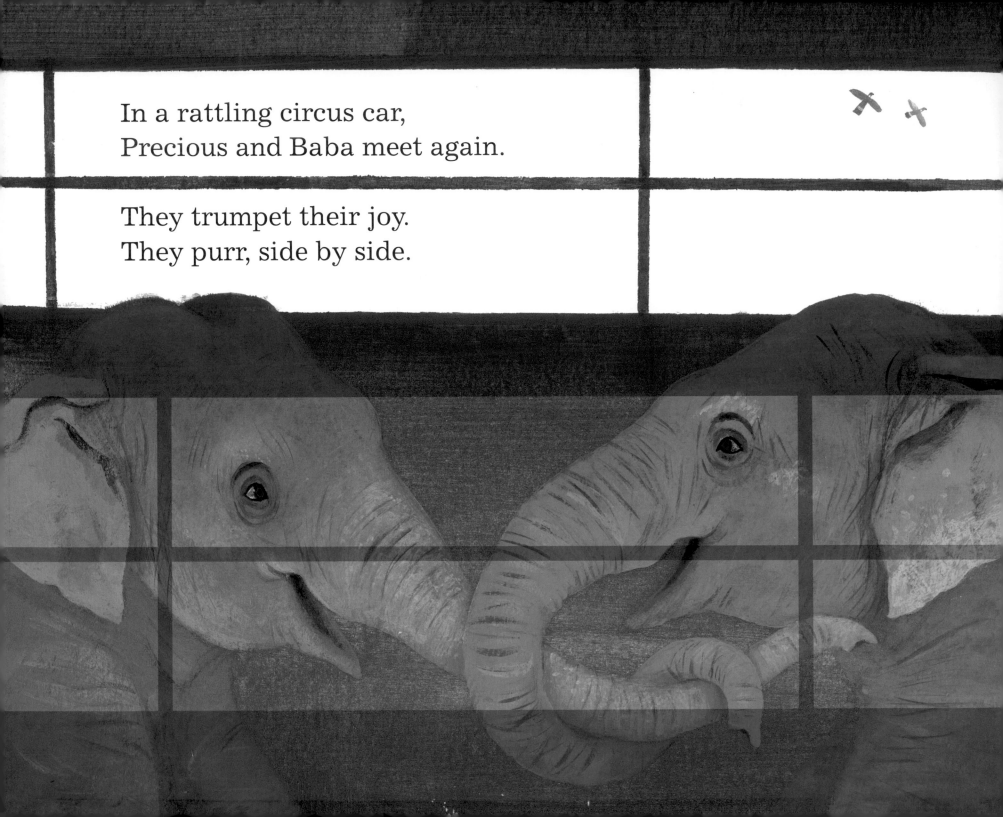

In a rattling circus car,
Precious and Baba meet again.

They trumpet their joy.
They purr, side by side.

The calves learn to climb on balls,
ride bikes,
and walk single file in the snow.

Precious makes mistakes.
Her knees begin to hurt.

At night,
Baba curls her trunk around Precious.

The trainers scare Baba.
Her ears ring with shouts
and commands.

At night,
Precious stands over her friend.

Under the big top,
corn pops,
whips crack,
and people clap.

Precious and Baba trot in a small circle,
lifting one leg
and then the other.
They blink their eyes.
*The lights are too bright!*
They shake their heads.
*The noise is too loud!*

Precious stumbles.
Baba cries out!
They charge to each other's side,
each protecting the other.
The circus is ruined.

"Time to sell Precious," says the trainer.
"And Baba."

Year after year,
Precious moves from zoo to zoo.

Decade after decade,
Baba lives circus to circus.

Precious stops walking.
Her feet hurt all the time.
She cries for Baba.

Baba stops talking.
Her throat aches.
She dreams of Precious.

At last, the director of the zoo examines Precious.
Her eyes are dull.
Her trunk, flat.
"I know of a place," he says.

He takes Precious to a sanctuary
where caretakers wash and feed her.
They bathe her feet with medicine.

After a time, she walks again.
The sun warms her back.
Her scars begin to heal.

But, still...
she misses Baba.

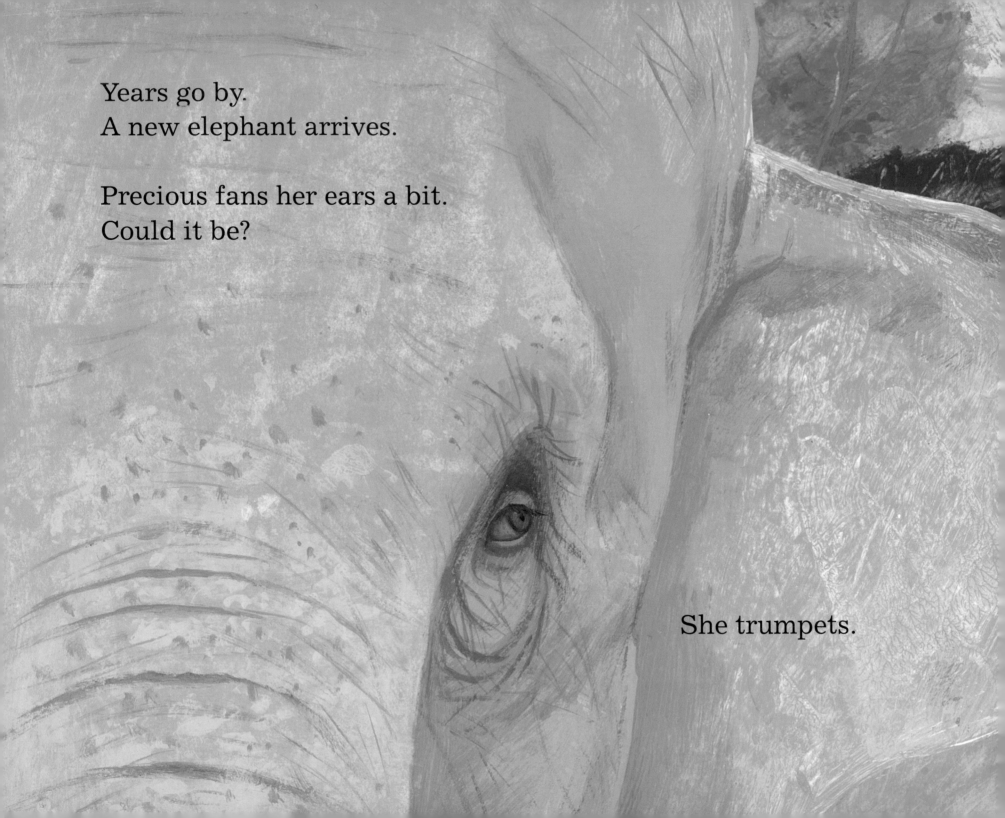

Years go by.
A new elephant arrives.

Precious fans her ears a bit.
Could it be?

She trumpets.

Baba purrs.

They stretch and curl their trunks
around each other,
then set off
to roam and forage.

Side by side
again.
Curious and proud
again.

Ten thousand stars shine
on Precious and Baba talking
and walking
together.

# Author's Note

**Elephant best friends? Yes.** The story of Precious and Baba is inspired by the true friendship of two Asian elephants that met in a circus. Real elephants, Gypsy and Wanda, were captured as calves and sold to the same circus. Records show that the elephants knew each other and performed together under difficult conditions. They were separated for twenty years until, old and sick, they reunited at the Performing Animal Welfare Society's sanctuary near San Andreas, California. When Gypsy moved into the Asian elephant barn, she headed straight for her old friend, Wanda. The two foraged and trumpeted side by side until Wanda's death in 2015.

There are only two species of elephants—the Asian elephant, which can weigh up to 5.5 tons, and its larger African elephant cousin, which can weigh up to 6 tons. The African elephant is the largest land mammal on Earth.

The majority of elephants in circuses and zoos today were born in the wild, where they lived and roamed with their families.

Wild elephants are active for about eighteen hours per day and can travel up to thirty miles during that time. They eat approximately 300 pounds of roots, grasses, trees, and bark per day, and come from places with hot climates, such as the Congo and Thailand. They like to toss dirt, play, roll in mud, and bathe in rivers.

Elephant trainers use bull hooks and whips to make captive elephants perform tricks, such as holding another elephant's tail or standing on another's back. Performing elephants often suffer from arthritis from walking on hard surfaces, and nightmares from being separated from their families, as well as sleeplessness, sadness, fear, and aggression.

It's not just captive elephants that are in danger. Farms and towns continue to take over the habitats of wild elephants, and poachers continue to kill these giants and harvest their ivory tusks. From 2003 to 2016, the wild elephant population in central Africa dropped by 64 percent. Poachers killed 100,000 elephants from 2009 to 2012 alone.

Do elephants need your help? Absolutely. Governments all over the world are collecting money to protect existing herds and prevent poaching. They depend on school and community support. Zoos are making an effort

too. Some have closed their elephant exhibits, and others support conservation efforts by promoting awareness and sponsoring education and research. Circuses are also changing. Public pressure led the popular Ringling Bros. and Barnum & Bailey Circus to end its elephant act in 2016, and in 2017 the circus closed completely.

To learn more about elephants and how to help these amazing animals, check out these programs and initiatives:

**International Elephant Foundation**

www.elephantconservation.org

**Los Angeles Zoo: Elephants of Asia**

www.lazoo.org/animals/elephantsofasia/

**Performing Animal Welfare Society**

www.pawsweb.org

**US Fish and Wildlife Service: Wildlife Without Borders**

www.fws.gov/international/wildlife-without-borders/

**World Elephant Day**

www.worldelephantday.org/about/elephants

Selected Sources

Ewinger, James. "Cleveland Metroparks Zoo Rebrands to Emphasize Conservation." *The Plain Dealer.* Last Modified March 17, 2017. http://www.cleveland.com/metro/index.ssf/2017/03/cleveland_metroparks_zoo_rebra.html

George Wittemyer, et al. "Illegal Killing for Ivory Drives Global Decline in African Elephants." *Proceedings of the National Academy of Sciences* 111, no. 36 (2014): 13117–13121. doi: 10.1073/pnas.1403984111

Hughes, Trevor. "Animal Rights Activists Claim Major Win in Ringling Bros. Closing." *USA Today.* Last modified January 15, 2017. https://www.usatoday.com/story/news/nation/2017/01/15/circus-closing-major-victory-animal-rights-activists/96614184/

"Meet the Elephants." *Performing Animal Welfare Society.* Accessed April 11, 2017. http://www.pawsweb.org/meet_elephants.html

Scriber, Brad. "100,000 Elephants Killed by Poachers in Just Three Years, Landmark Analysis Finds." *National Geographic.* Last modified August 18, 2014. http://news.nationalgeographic.com/news/2014/08/140818-elephants-africa-poaching-cites-census/

To MM, with love—CLM

For Miglena, my best friend—BM

Library of Congress Cataloging-in-Publication data is on file with the publisher.

Text copyright © 2017 by Cheryl Lawton Malone
Pictures copyright © 2017 by Albert Whitman & Company
Pictures by Bistra Masseva
Published in 2017 by Albert Whitman & Company
ISBN 978-0-8075-1960-8

Printed in China
10  9  8  7  6  5  4  3  2  1  HH  22  21  20  19  18  17

Design by Jordan Kost

For more information about Albert Whitman & Company,
visit our website at www.albertwhitman.com.